Withdrawn

HARRY
HORNACRE

by Jennifer Dizmang Illustrated by Mark Ludy

Saves
for
a
Bike

Was
picking
up poo
for
Mr.
Beeline.

All his
friends
laughed cuz'
they thought it
was funny

That Harry would
work so hard to earn
all his money

But Harry
didn't care
as he
turned out
the light

Cuz' he knew he was saving
for his fancy new bike

How happy he was
when the last penny was earned

A valuable lesson
that he had learned

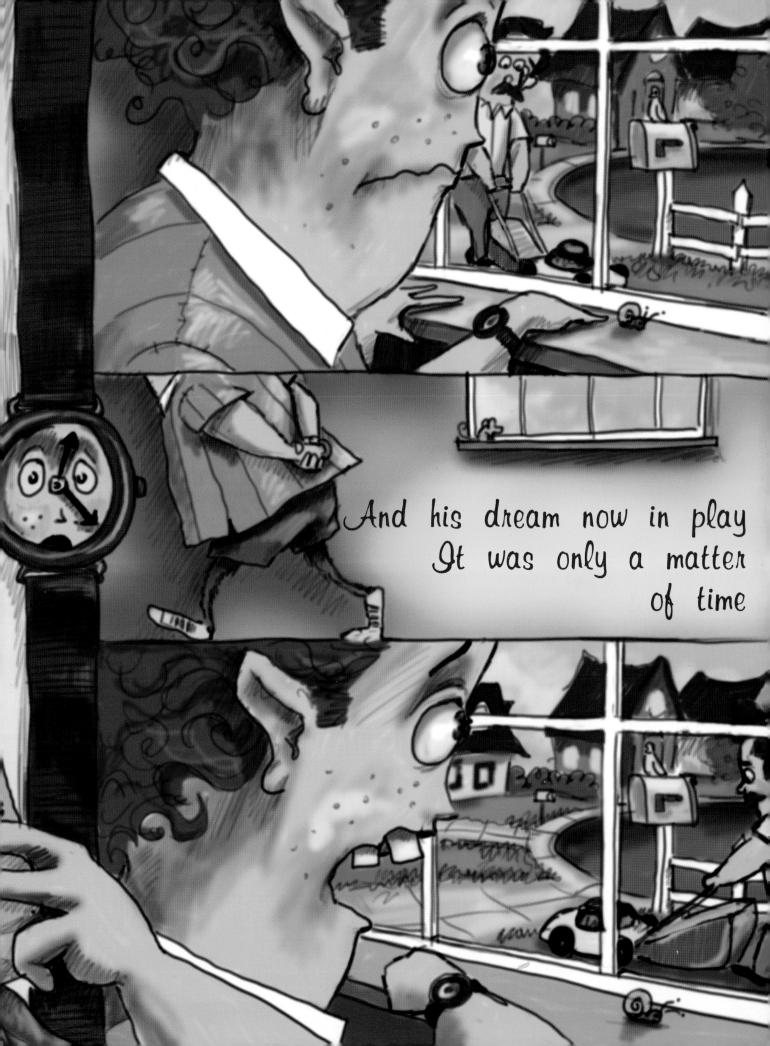

And his dream now in play
It was only a matter
of time

His mom was right

Hold your dream tight

And everything
will turn out fine

And you could hear the "oohs and aahs"
as he rode out of sight

The wind in his hair

And Molly alongside

Reminded Harry it was worth saving
for this really cool ride

THE
END